Second Chances

by Erin Falligant

illustrated by Arcana Studios

★ American Girl®

Published by American Girl Publishing
Copyright © 2013 by American Girl

Questions or comments? Call 1-800-845-0005,
visit **americangirl.com**, or write to Customer Service,
American Girl, 8400 Fairway Place, Middleton, WI 53562-0497.

Printed in China
13 14 15 16 17 18 19 20 LEO 10 9 8 7 6 5 4 3 2 1

Illustrated by Thu Thai at Arcana Studios

Welcome to Innerstar University! At this imaginary, one-of-a-kind school, you can live with your friends in a dorm called Brightstar House and find lots of fun ways to let your true talents shine. Your friends at Innerstar U will help you find your way through some challenging situations, too.

When you reach a page in this book that asks you to make a decision, choose carefully. The decisions you make will lead to more than 20 different endings! (*Hint:* Use a pencil to check off your choices. That way, you'll never read the same story twice.)

Want to try another ending? Read the book again—and then again. Find out what would have happened if you'd made *different* choices. Then head to www.innerstarU.com for even more book endings, games, and fun with friends.

Innerstar Guides

Every girl needs a few good friends to help her find her way. These are the friends who are always there for **you**.

Emmy

A brave girl who loves swimming and boating

Isabel

A confident girl with a funky sense of style

Riley

A good sport, on the field and off

Paige

A nature lover who leads hikes and campus cleanups

Amber

An animal lover and
a loyal friend

Neely

A creative girl who loves
dance, music, and art

Logan

A super-smart girl
who is curious about
EVERYTHING

Shelby

A kind girl who is there
for her friends—and loves
making NEW friends!

Innerstar U Campus

1. Rising Star Stables
2. Star Student Center
3. Brightstar House
4. Starlight Library
5. Sparkle Studios
6. Blue Sky Nature Center

7. Real Spirit Center
8. Five-Points Plaza
9. Starfire Lake & Boathouse
10. U-Shine Hall
11. Good Sports Center
12. Shopping Square
13. The Market
14. Morningstar Meadow

[**S**] ummer has settled over Innerstar University, but it sure doesn't feel like summer to you. While your friends are packing suitcases to head home for the break, *you're* packing your backpack for your first day of summer school.

You broke your leg in the spring and missed classes, so you have to stay behind at Innerstar U this summer to make up work. You're so depressed. You can't believe your friends are leaving you for *two whole months.*

"Amber is staying," your friend Shelby reminds you as she zips up her suitcase. She wheels it toward the door, where Megan and Logan are waiting.

"Amber's great!" says Logan, holding the door open for Shelby. "You'll have fun hanging out with her."

Turn to page 10.

You agree—Amber is a lot of fun. But she's staying behind to volunteer at Pet-Palooza, a pet day-care center that's crazy busy in the summer. You're pretty sure that Amber won't have much time to spend with you.

"Don't forget about Jamie," says Megan with a sly smile.

You roll your eyes. You've known Jamie for a long time, but you're not exactly friends. She's one of those girls who's always playing tricks on people and cracking jokes that only *she* thinks are funny.

"Remember what a pain she was on the diving team?" asks Megan. "She was always hiding someone's duffel bag or doing cannonballs instead of practicing."

"Remember how she tried to ruin our bean-plant experiment?" adds Logan. Nothing irks Logan more than someone messing with the facts.

Shelby fiddles with the handle of her suitcase. You remember how Jamie teased her when she found out Shelby couldn't swim, which was a pretty mean thing to do. If anyone should be annoyed with Jamie, it's Shelby, but she's too nice to say so.

"Jamie's not always like that," she says instead. "Who knows? She might surprise you."

 Turn to page 12.

As you walk your friends down the hall to the lobby of Brightstar House, you think about Shelby's words: *Jamie might surprise you.* And sure enough, as you step into the lobby, she does. Jamie leaps out from behind a big plant and says, "Hey!"

Beneath her brown bangs, Jamie's eyes carry a glint of pride. Nothing seems to bring her more joy than making people jump out of their skin.

Ignoring the irritated look on Megan's face, Jamie falls into step beside you. "What classes did you sign up for this summer?" she asks.

You're reluctant to tell her. Usually, the less information you give Jamie, the better. But you have to say something, or she'll keep pestering you.

 If you tell Jamie what classes you're taking, turn to page 16.

If you change the subject, turn to page 14.

You raise your pointer finger, letting Jamie know that you'll be just a minute—you have to get a drink of water. What you really need is time to figure out how to handle this. If you're going to be in class with Jamie every day, you need a game plan.

You stall at the fountain until your volleyball teacher calls everyone to attention. Then you plop down on the gym floor behind a group of girls you don't know.

What you quickly find out is that every passing and setting drill the teacher has planned for you involves a partner, and you don't have one of those—at least not a partner you know. You end up partnering with a girl named Maggie, who doesn't waste any time telling you that she's the best player on her club volleyball team back home in Oregon.

 Turn to page 21.

"I can't talk right now," you say to Jamie. "I have to help these guys catch their bus."

As you push past Jamie, you reach down to help Shelby with one of her duffel bags. The bus doesn't actually come for another ten minutes, but if you and your friends hide out in the far corner of the lobby, maybe Jamie won't find you there.

Before you hug your friends good-bye, you make sure they all have your e-mail address. You know Shelby will e-mail you a lot—she's good about that. But Megan will be traveling, and Logan? She'll probably have her nose stuck in a book or two—or twelve—and won't come up for air until August.

As your friends board the bus, you feel a lump of loneliness in your stomach. What a rotten way to start summer vacation.

 Turn to page 17.

You quickly rattle off the three summer-school classes you're taking: English, history, and volleyball. Then you brace yourself, waiting for Jamie to make some crack about your choices. And she does.

"English and history? BOR-ing," she says, following up her words with an exaggerated yawn. "But volleyball's cool. Maybe I'll sign up, too."

You stifle a groan—at least until Jamie walks away.

Shelby catches your eye and reads your mind, as usual. "It'll be *fine*," she insists, throwing her arm around your shoulders. "I'll e-mail you, and you can tell me all about it."

"And I'll send you pictures from my trip," adds Megan, who's heading to Florida with her family.

"Thanks," you say to your friends. Your heart feels heavy as you say good-bye to them, but knowing you can stay in touch through e-mail makes things a little bit better.

 Turn to page 18.

You don't feel any better on Monday morning, when you're sitting in English class and already have your first assignment: an essay about something that makes you laugh. It's supposed to be fun, and maybe it would be if it weren't due this Friday. Your teacher says that you'll have an essay due *every* week this summer. Yikes!

To top that off, you get an assignment in history, too—you have to read the first chapter of your book by tomorrow.

And volleyball, which is the class you've been looking forward to all morning, turns out to be really lonely. You walk into the gym a few minutes early and don't see anyone you know, so you sit down on the bleachers and pull out your history book. Might as well get started on that reading.

"Hey," someone says from behind you.

You glance up and see a curly-haired girl reading a book of her own a few rows up.

"I hear we need to find a partner for the drills," she says in a friendly tone. "Do you want to be partners?"

You smile and nod. You're grateful for the invitation, and Kelsey looks nice enough. You can't help wishing that she were Shelby, though. You miss your friends!

 Turn to page 22.

On Monday morning, campus seems almost empty as you walk to your first class: English. There are a few girls there who look sort of familiar, and a few others who must be coming to Innerstar U just for the summer. Nobody looks your way as you walk in, so you choose a seat near the front of the classroom and busy yourself unpacking your backpack.

Your second class, history, is pretty lonely, too. You're so used to being surrounded by friends in class that you forgot what it was like to be the new girl—or the odd girl out.

By the time you get to the volleyball court at the Good Sports Center, you're feeling pretty blue. It's going to be a l-o-n-g summer if you have to spend it all alone. So when Jamie waves to you and motions for you to come sit by her on the bleachers, you're *almost* tempted.

⭐ If you sit by Jamie, turn to page 20.

⭐ If you stall for time, turn to page 13.

You find yourself walking toward Jamie. She can be a pain, for sure, but she looks genuinely happy to see you. And it's only for one class, right? If Jamie's too annoying, you can always avoid her tomorrow.

"Hey, partner!" she says as you take a seat beside her.

The word *partner* makes you cringe, but as class starts and you move from bumping drills to serving drills, Jamie turns out to be a pretty good partner.

Jamie is one of the few girls in class who can serve a volleyball overhand. You're a *terrible* server, but Jamie gives you some pointers and keeps you laughing, which makes the hour go by quickly. And when it's your turn at the service line, she makes funny faces at you—which some-how helps you relax and actually get the ball over the net.

 Turn to page 24.

You want to ask Maggie what a pro like her is doing in an intermediate volleyball course, but you don't. Instead, you try to keep your eyes focused on the ball, which Maggie is sending at you really fast.

She's supposed to toss it, and you're supposed to gently bump it back. That's a hard thing to do when her toss is more like a fast pitch. The ball bounces off your forearms and flies sideways, messing up two other players who are doing the drill next to you.

"Girls, please try to stay in control of the ball," your teacher calls to you from the sidelines.

Maggie must think that scolding is directed only at you, because she gives you a superior look before hurling the ball your way again.

 Turn to page 26.

You and Kelsey don't talk very much in between volleyball drills or after class. It's hard to get to know someone new. You just don't know if you have the energy today.

After volleyball, you grab a quick lunch and head back to your room. You slump down in your desk chair, trying to figure out what to write about for your English essay. You can't think of anything that makes you laugh—not one thing. You decide to walk around campus looking for inspiration, but it's amazing how *not* funny life can be when you're actually looking for the humor in it.

You wander through the Market, which is full of girls shopping and chatting with friends. When you reach Morningstar Meadow, something catches your eye—a girl taking a puppy for a walk. You can tell by the girl's dark braids that it's Amber.

As you get closer, you see that the *puppy* is actually taking *Amber* for the walk. And it's a puppy you've never seen before, a stout little dog with a huge head and a smushed-in face.

When Amber sees you, she waves and jogs your way. "This is Meatloaf," she says, urging the pup to stop and sit. "He's an English bulldog."

Meatloaf? Now *that's* funny! You think you just met the subject of your first essay.

Turn to page 25.

The next day in volleyball class, you partner up again with Jamie—and the day after that. You surprise yourself by having a pretty good time with her. Still, there's this voice in your head that says *Careful. You know how Jamie can be. Don't trust her.*

On Thursday afternoon as you're walking out of the gym, Jamie catches you off-guard with a question: "Hey, do you want to eat with me tonight at the student center?"

"Um . . . sure," you say—without even thinking.

But as you part ways in front of the sports center, you start to worry and wonder. *Does Jamie think we're friends now? Are we?*

Given your history with Jamie, you're not sure how you feel about a friendship with her. You need some advice—fast. And you know just the person to ask. You quicken your step as you walk the stone path back toward your dorm room.

As soon as you step inside your room, you dump your duffel on the floor and sit down in front of your computer. You send Shelby an e-mail with a subject line that reads "Help!" Shelby is usually pretty wise about situations like this.

 Turn to page 28.

You tell Amber about your assignment, and she laughs. "Meatloaf will make a great subject," she agrees. "He's kind of *my* assignment, too. His owners are hoping we can teach him some manners."

Amber explains that bulldogs are sometimes hard to train. "They're stubborn and hard-headed," she says. "Meatloaf just wants to do things his way."

You squat down to pet Meatloaf. Just looking at his cute face cracks you up. He has a pushed-in little nose, a wrinkly forehead, and a serious underbite. His lower jaw juts forward, which means his bottom teeth and the tip of his pink tongue are always showing, especially when he pants.

"What a great face!" you say, scratching Meatloaf behind the ears. "Can I bring my camera sometime and take pictures of him?"

Turn to page 29.

The spiking drill doesn't go well, either. Maggie is supposed to hit the ball hard toward the ground, and you're supposed to toss the ball back to her. She hits the ball hard all right—directly at your face.

While you're holding your nose, wondering if it's going to bleed, Maggie apologizes. But as she adjusts her knee pads, you hear her mumble something about you being kind of a baby.

A funny thing happens then. Jamie is walking by to fill up her water bottle, and she must have seen the whole thing, because she picks up the volleyball and pretends to throw it toward Maggie's face. She doesn't let go of the ball, but Maggie still panics. She ducks and squeals, and then she gives Jamie the dirtiest of looks.

"Well, how do *you* like it?" Jamie asks Maggie. Then she hands the ball to you and keeps walking.

You've been on the other side of Jamie's rudeness plenty of times, but today she was *defending* you instead of teasing you. You're not quite sure what to do with that.

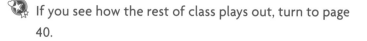 If you follow Jamie to thank her, turn to page 37.

If you see how the rest of class plays out, turn to page 40.

You check your in-box every two minutes, and when you hear the *ding* of incoming mail, you leap back in front of your desk. The e-mail is from Shelby, who suddenly doesn't seem quite so far away. And just as you had hoped, she has some great advice:

It's okay to hang out with Jamie, as long as she's being nice. That doesn't mean you're best friends or anything. It would take a while for you to really trust Jamie, right? But it's good that you're slowly giving her a chance.

Shelby's advice makes you feel a ton better. That feeling stays with you as you change your clothes and get ready for dinner with Jamie.

But early the following week, when Jamie asks if you want to plan a sleepover for the weekend, you don't know what to do. *A sleepover?* You're not sure you're ready to hang out with her for *that* much time. But she's looking at you with such a hopeful face. What do you say?

If you say yes, turn to page 34.

If you say no, turn to page 32.

Amber nods. "Can you come tomorrow?" she asks. "I'll be working with Meatloaf here in the meadow every day after lunch."

"Sure—" you start to say.

"Sounds like fun!" a familiar voice calls from behind you. "Can I come, too?"

You whirl around and see Jamie, who seems to have materialized out of thin air. She has a knack for that, you've noticed.

Amber hesitates for just a second before saying, "Be my guest. The more, the merrier."

Ack! You wish Amber hadn't agreed to that. You give her a look that says as much, and she raises her palm slightly at her side as if to say, *What was I supposed to do?*

You know that Amber was in an awkward spot, and now you are, too. Will you meet up in the meadow again with Amber and Meatloaf if it means spending time with Jamie, too?

 If you head to the meadow the next day, turn to page 30.

 If you decide not to go, turn to page 41.

You've already said yes to hanging out with Amber and Meatloaf tomorrow, so you guess you're hanging out with Jamie, too.

On Tuesday after lunch, you walk toward the meadow. You spot Amber instantly, and when Meatloaf sees you, he starts tugging at his leash. Amber finally lets go of the leash and lets him run to you.

Meatloaf waddle-runs across the grass on his short little legs, and by the time he reaches you, he's breathing so hard that he's snorting. You giggle and reach down to pet him, getting a hand full of drool.

"Gross!" Jamie calls from behind you. "I guess I won't be shaking your hand today."

Ugh. You were hoping that you and Amber would have a few minutes alone for Meatloaf's photo shoot, but no such luck. You try to hide your disappointment as you wipe your hand clean in the grass.

Later, as you try to take photos of Meatloaf, Jamie keeps distracting him by clowning around behind you. You take one bad shot after another and then finally give up.

I guess I'll try again tomorrow, you think—but you don't say that out loud. You don't want Jamie to show up again and ruin things.

 Turn to page 33.

You make up an excuse for not being able to sleep over at Jamie's. "I have to work on my English paper all weekend," you say.

Jamie seems suspicious about that, but she doesn't say anything—until the following weekend. You're walking through the Market when she extends another invitation: "Do you want to watch the campus fireworks down by the lake with me on Saturday? Then maybe afterward we could have a sleepover."

You're torn. You've never seen the fireworks here at Innerstar U, and you'd like to. But you don't want to do a sleepover with Jamie—you're just not ready to spend that much time with her. So you muster up another excuse.

"I have to study for a history quiz Saturday," you say. It's sort of true, but not entirely.

"*All* weekend?" Jamie says, her eyes locked with yours. "Wow, I thought you were more fun than that. I guess I was wrong."

Here we go, you think. You and Jamie had a few good weeks together, but now things are going back to normal—and normal between you and Jamie is *not* good.

 If you say something nasty back, turn to page 36.

 If you ask Jamie why she has to be mean about it, turn to page 47.

But what if Jamie does *show up again tomorrow?* you worry on the walk back to your room. It's a free country, after all—you can't control where she goes and doesn't go.

It's moments like this when you really miss your friend Shelby, who always has great advice for how to deal with difficult people like Jamie. You decide to e-mail Shelby and tell her all about the Meatloaf/Jamie situation.

You're thrilled to get a response from Shelby just before bedtime. But instead of advice about Jamie, all Shelby can talk about is Meatloaf. *A bulldog?* she writes. *I'm terrified of them. Aren't they supposed to be really mean?*

Shelby's totally missing the point of your e-mail, but you answer her question anyway.

I think bulldogs just have a bad reputation, you write. *Amber says Meatloaf is stubborn and hard-headed, but he's actually a sweetheart when you get to know him.*

You send the e-mail and wait, but Shelby never writes back with advice about Jamie. What do you do?

 If you try to beat Jamie to the meadow on Wednesday, turn to page 38.

 If you decide not to go back, turn to page 41.

Jamie seems so excited about a sleepover that you don't know how to say no. Saturday night, you grab your sleeping bag and duffel and head over to her room.

You're surprised to see that Jamie's room is filled with butterfly *everything*—mobiles, posters, and more. "I love butterflies," she says in kind of an embarrassed voice. "Check this out—I have a pet caterpillar, too."

It takes you a moment to spot the green caterpillar climbing the leaf in the corner of the aquarium.

"That's Harriet," says Jamie. "I think she's going to turn into a California Sister butterfly."

"Cool," you say, though you have no idea what a California Sister butterfly looks like.

 Turn to page 39.

You could take the high road, but why bother? Jamie is Jamie. You might as well fight back.

"And I thought you were more *nice* than that," you say to her. "I guess I was wrong, too."

Jamie's eyes flash. "Whatever," she says sharply before turning and disappearing into a crowd of girls.

After that, things are tense at volleyball. Jamie stays on the other side of the gym, which means you both have to partner up with girls you don't really know. Your serves take a nosedive without Jamie's tips and jokes to relax you. And you're not having nearly as much fun anymore.

You keep replaying that last conversation with Jamie in your mind. "I thought you were more nice than that," you'd said to Jamie. But all Jamie had done was invite you to a couple of sleepovers. That *was* being nice, wasn't it? A lot nicer than pretending to be busy with schoolwork, which was what you did.

You try to convince yourself that it's better this way— that you and Jamie never *really* would have become friends. But as you watch her having fun with a new girl on the volleyball court, you wonder. Unfortunately, now you'll never know.

The End

You catch up with Jamie at the water fountain. "Thanks for that," you say. Your voice sounds funny because you're still holding your nose.

"No problem," says Jamie. "What are friends for?"

Friends? You're speechless.

"Hey, you're bleeding!" Jamie says, pointing toward your nose. Sure enough, when you take your hand away, you see a smear of blood.

Your volleyball teacher sees it, too. She quickly brings you a towel and leads you toward a bench. While you tilt your head and pinch your nose shut, Jamie sits beside you. She must think it's her job to entertain you, because she gives you a play-by-play of everything going on in the gym.

"Uh-oh. Maggie's partnering up with *my* old partner now," she says. "I hope she doesn't take out another player with that machine-gun arm of hers. The girl shouldn't even be allowed on the court!"

Jamie is talking loudly—too loudly—and you glance up, hoping no one heard her. But you figure that Jamie's still kind of defending you, in her own way. And a few minutes later, when you take the towel away from your nose to see if the bleeding has stopped, Jamie seems genuinely interested and concerned.

 Turn to page 42.

On Wednesday, you hurry to the meadow before lunch in the hope of catching Amber before Jamie shows up. Amber isn't there, so you walk across the meadow to Pet-Palooza.

Amber is sitting behind the front desk. She can't take you to see Meatloaf because she's on desk duty, but she answers your questions while she works.

You write down *lots* of things about bulldogs:

- They're strong, but they're not very active (because it's hard to take in air through their smushed-in noses!).
- They can't swim well, but they can be taught cool tricks like skateboarding.
- They can be mischievous and destructive but usually because they're looking for attention.
- They're total clowns that will do anything to make you laugh.
- They're super faithful and protective of their owners and families.
- They're called "bullies" for short. Ha!

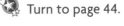 Turn to page 44.

You watch the caterpillar for a while and then look at the other things on Jamie's desk. She doesn't have many pictures up, except for a photo of the diving team and a framed family photo. When you look closely at that, you realize that Jamie has a lot of older brothers—all dark-haired, like her and her mom.

Next to the family photo is a worn-out stuffed crocodile. You lift it up, and it flops over sideways in your hand. That crocodile has seen a lot of love, you can tell.

"Hey, easy with that!" says Jamie, reaching for the crocodile. "That's Cuddles, my oldest friend."

Cuddles? You stifle a giggle. It's hard to imagine tough, wisecracking Jamie cuddling with anything.

In her room, though, Jamie seems shy and awkward. She asks what you want to do, and when you ask her what she normally likes to do at sleepovers, she just shrugs. It occurs to you then that a girl like Jamie probably doesn't go to a lot of sleepovers.

 Turn to page 46.

What Jamie did for you was nice, but she could just as easily have teased you about getting a ball in the face. You never know with that girl. So you tend to your nose (which is bleeding now) and hope for a better class tomorrow.

Unfortunately, the next day is even worse. You have to do drills with Maggie again because everyone else is already partnered up—even Jamie, who seems to be having fun with some red-haired girl.

You're doing a serving drill, and you can't seem to get the ball over the net. Your first serve goes straight into the net. The next serve veers wildly to the right and misses the court altogether.

"Keep trying," your teacher says.

But you hear an exaggerated sigh from Maggie, who is in line right behind you.

So you do the weak thing. You grab your stomach and say to your teacher, "Can I take a quick break? My stomach hurts."

 Turn to page 43.

The next morning, you decide *not* to go back to Morningstar Meadow. Jamie will just ruin things again, and besides, you can get all the facts you need about bulldogs from the Internet, right?

After classes end, you head to your room and cozy up in front of the computer. You jot down a bunch of facts about bulldogs:

- In Spain and England during the 1600s and 1700s, bulldogs were used as working dogs on farms.
- Bulldogs used to guard cattle—even bulls, which is how they got their name!
- Bulldogs are still the national dog of England.
- Bulldogs are called "bullies" for short. Ha!

It takes about an hour to write your essay. You even drop in a photo of a bulldog you found online. Then you print the final version. You're pretty proud of it!

 Turn to page 45.

After practice ends, you walk out of the sports center with Jamie. "Hey," she says, pulling her duffel onto her shoulder, "do you want to be partners in class tomorrow?"

You hesitate. An hour ago, you chose not to partner up with Jamie because you know how annoying she can be. But she showed another side of herself today, and frankly, *either* side of Jamie has got to be better than Maggie. So you say yes.

The next day, you meet Jamie at the court, and you end up having a pretty good time with your new partner. At first, she messes around a lot. She bumps the ball with her legs spread wide, as if she were throwing a basketball "granny style," and she pretends to miss the ball every time she gears up for a spike.

But you can tell that Jamie is actually a decent volleyball player. She even gives you some tips for how to improve your serve. And the best news? With Jamie as your partner, there are no bloody noses involved. *Success*, you think to yourself as you head to the locker room to change your clothes.

 Turn to page 24.

The next day, the thought of playing volleyball *does* make you sick to your stomach, so you skip class. And the day after that? You stay in your room again. You just can't bear the thought of going back.

You end up dropping out of volleyball. You signed up for it thinking it would be your fun class this summer, but as it turns out, you'll have a lot more fun in English and history than playing volleyball in a gym full of strangers and with a partner like Maggie.

You run into Jamie a couple of times over the summer, and she asks why you're not doing volleyball anymore. She seems genuinely disappointed. You flash back to that moment when she stood up for you during class, and you wonder how things might have gone if you'd partnered with Jamie instead of Maggie. Would you still be in volleyball? Would you and Jamie have gotten along? You'll never know.

As you start counting the days till the end of summer, you can't help feeling as if you missed out on something during these last few weeks. But you can't go back now.

The End

"Wow, Amber," you say, glancing back over your list. "Thanks for the info. I think I have plenty of material for my essay!"

"No worries," says Amber. "But does that mean you won't be joining me and Meatloaf after lunch?" She sounds disappointed.

You don't want Amber to think that you don't want to hang out with *her* today, so you tell her the truth. "I'm just not that crazy about the idea of spending more time with Jamie," you admit.

Amber nods knowingly. "It's tough," she agrees. "Jamie is a little bit like Meatloaf. She's hard-headed and will do *anything* for a laugh."

That makes you giggle—and feel a little sorry for Meatloaf, who you don't think is much like Jamie at all.

"Maybe," Amber goes on, "Jamie just needs someone to pay her some attention. Did you know that she's the youngest of eight kids, and she's the only girl?"

 Turn to page 51.

You turn in your essay on Thursday, a day early. Your teacher looks impressed by your timeliness and says she'll have your essay back to you by Friday. You can't wait!

But Friday morning, you're less than impressed with your final grade: B–. Your teacher wrote this comment on the top of the page: "Interesting facts about bulldogs. But the assignment was to write about something that makes you laugh. What about bulldogs makes you laugh?"

Oops. You forgot the whole point of the essay!

Meatloaf definitely makes you laugh, but writing about Meatloaf is way different from writing about bulldogs that lived four hundred years ago.

I deserve the grade I got, you think with a sigh.

 Turn to page 52.

After you unroll your sleeping bags on the floor and put in a funny DVD to watch, Jamie laughs and starts acting less shy. Just before she turns out the light, she reaches for Cuddles and tucks the crocodile gently into her sleeping bag.

You're tempted to make a joke. The old Jamie would have teased you and probably called you a baby for sleeping with a stuffed animal, after all. But you say nothing.

After the sleepover, you find yourself wondering a lot about Jamie—about how different she seems at home in her room from when she's out on campus, and about how different she seems this summer from how she usually is during the school year.

You like this new Jamie, but is she for real? And if she can be so fun and so nice, why isn't she that way all the time?

You wish you could just ask Jamie those questions, but you're getting along so well now, you don't want to mess things up. Still . . . you wish you understood her better.

 If you find a way to ask Jamie your questions, turn to page 53.

 If you keep them to yourself, turn to page 48.

"Why do you have to be mean about it?" you ask Jamie, trying to keep your voice steady. "I thought we were having a lot of fun this summer."

Jamie stares at you for a moment, and her eyes lose some of their fire. She shrugs and says, "I thought we were having fun, too. So why don't you want to do a sleepover with me?" She suddenly looks more hurt than mad.

This time, you realize, you owe her the truth. You take a deep breath. "Because it's hard for me to trust you, Jamie," you say. "You've been so fun to be around this summer, but during the school year you said and did a lot of not-very-nice things."

Jamie opens her mouth to protest. She's gearing up for a fight, but you see the moment when she decides to let it go. She turns her face away from yours, and the two of you keep walking—out of the Market and past the lake—in silence.

 Turn to page 50.

You don't ask Jamie any awkward questions. You don't want to put her on the spot. But you find yourself watching her closely at volleyball class, and you make an interesting observation: When it's just the two of you doing passing or setting drills, she's really fun. But when you're playing a game with *all* the girls, you see the old Jamie now and then.

One Wednesday afternoon, you're playing a game, and your teacher keeps reminding both sides to try to hit the ball at least twice before sending it back over the net. Jamie is on your team, and you can tell she's getting frustrated because no one is passing the ball to her.

"I was *right* there, ready for the ball," Jamie says to one of your teammates. "Are you blind or what?"

After that Jamie starts doing silly things, such as hitting the ball right back over on the first hit or bumping the ball as hard as she can so that it hits the gym ceiling.

You're afraid the volleyball teacher is going to pull Jamie out of the game. What do you do?

 If you take Jamie aside to ask her what's going on, turn to page 54.

 If you try to include her more in the game, turn to page 58.

As you pass Starlight Library, Jamie suddenly stops walking and sinks down on a bench. She looks up at you with wet eyes and absolute sincerity in her face. You almost don't recognize this girl.

"I don't know why I do things that upset people," she says in a small voice, shrugging. "I guess I just figure that everyone is always mad at me anyway."

Then you hear something you never thought you'd hear Jamie say—the words "I'm sorry."

Her apology hangs in the air for a moment, and you feel something shift inside you. By the time you sit down beside Jamie, you've already forgiven her.

"Jamie," you say, breaking the awkward silence, "I'd like to go to the fireworks with you, if you still want to."

You don't mention the sleepover, because you're still not sure you want to do that. But just going to the fireworks seems okay with Jamie. She smiles and wipes her face with the back of her hand. "I'd like that," she says.

 Turn to page 56.

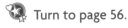

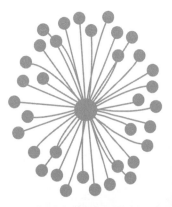

Your jaw drops. "Jamie has *seven* brothers? How in the world do you know that?" you ask.

Amber shrugs. "I asked her once, I guess," she says. "You should try to get to know Jamie a little bit better, too. Before you judge someone or something, you should always get the facts." She grins and adds, "You can put that in your notes, if you want."

"Oh, I will!" you say. You pretend to scribble the quote down quickly in your notes. You're laughing, but you actually think Amber's words are pretty wise.

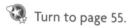 Turn to page 55.

Before you judge someone, get the facts.

The thought of your essay grade weighs on you throughout history and volleyball. After lunch, you decide to walk toward the meadow to see if Amber and Meatloaf are outside. Sure enough, they are—and Jamie's with them. It looks as if they're playing kickball, and Meatloaf is the outfielder.

At first you're annoyed to see Jamie. After all, if it hadn't been for her, you would have hung out with Amber and Meatloaf and gotten a better grade on your essay.

But the more you watch Amber and Jamie, who seem to be having a blast together, the more you realize how unfair you're being. Jamie didn't ruin your essay. *You* did. You were so set on steering clear of Jamie that you avoided Amber and Meatloaf, too. And by the looks of things, you missed out on more than just good material for your "what makes me laugh" essay. You also missed out on a pretty good time.

When Amber sees you, she waves and invites you to join her, Jamie, and Meatloaf. And this time, you say yes.

The End

You decide to talk to Jamie about how you're feeling, but how can you ask her some pretty awkward questions without hurting her feelings or making her angry?

Shelby to the rescue. If anyone can ask tough questions in a super-sweet way, she's the one.

You send Shelby another quick e-mail, and she must be online, because her reply pops up on-screen in a matter of minutes. Phew! She writes:

Just focus on the positive stuff. Tell Jamie that you're having a lot of fun with her now and that you wish you could get along this well all *the time.*

Perfect. You print out Shelby's e-mail so that you can practice the words. Then you wait for the right moment, which comes after a volleyball game at the sports center. Jamie played really well, so she's flying high. As you walk back to Brightstar House, you toss a volleyball back and forth.

"You know, Jamie," you say, your voice cracking a little, "I've had a lot of fun with you lately."

Jamie blushes and grins. "Me, too, partner," she says, tapping the ball playfully against your shoulder. And then there's an awkward silence. Here comes the hard part.

Turn to page 62.

You raise your hand and ask your teacher if you can all take a quick water break. At the fountain, you say to Jamie, "Why are you acting like this? You're going to get pulled out of the game."

Jamie shrugs off your warning. "Who cares?" she says. "This is boring anyway."

That makes you mad. You're tempted to say something mean back to Jamie, but you don't. You take a deep breath and try to keep your voice steady. "*I* care," you say to Jamie. "You and I have been practicing hard, and you've been a great partner. Why are things different during a game?"

Jamie's face softens. She seems pleased with the word *partner*. "I don't know," she says. "I guess partnering with you is a lot more fun than being in a game, where everyone leaves me out."

You want to argue that point. You're pretty sure that no one is purposely leaving Jamie out. But she obviously feels that way, and you know now that when she *feels* left out, she starts to act badly.

You can't control how your other teammates treat Jamie, but you can control what *you* do. So you say, "How about this: Let's pretend that we're doing drills. If you get the first ball, pass it to me. If I get the first ball, I'll pass it to you. Deal?"

Jamie grins. "You're on," she says.

Turn to page 63.

During lunch, you keep thinking about what Amber said: "Get the facts." You wonder what else you don't know about Jamie. And you start to get a little bit curious.

You head back to Morningstar Meadow after lunch to take photos of Meatloaf, and you're not all that surprised— or disappointed—to see Jamie there, rough-housing with Meatloaf. She jogs left and right while he chases her, snorting all the way.

Amber is there, too, and she looks thrilled to see you. She waves at you as she shakes a bag of treats, her signal to Meatloaf that it's time for him to settle down and run back to her.

As you set up your camera, you try to figure out a game plan. You know it's going to be tough to take pictures of Meatloaf with Jamie riling him up, but maybe you can use this opportunity to get to know her better.

 If you ask Amber to photograph Meatloaf while you talk with Jamie, turn to page 59.

 If you ask Jamie to pose with Meatloaf in your pictures, turn to page 60.

Saturday night, you and Jamie are sprawled on beach blankets along the grassy lakeshore. You're lying on your back, watching the explosions of color in the dark sky above.

Each sparkling shower is more beautiful than the last. An enormous purple flower bursts open overhead and sprouts blue swizzles punctuated by pops of gold. Jamie claps from the blanket beside you.

You glance over at Jamie's happy face. *Will we become friends?* you wonder. You're not sure yet. But you're willing to forgive the past and give Jamie a fresh start. And so far? So good.

The End

You try to keep Jamie's head in the game. Whenever the ball comes to you, you pass it to her. And Jamie starts playing more seriously again. When your team makes the winning point, she gives you a high-five and a broad smile.

As the two of you leave the court, it occurs to you that you just learned something about Jamie. You learned that when she's acting like a jerk, she's probably feeling bored or a little left out. Usually you ignore her when she's acting like that, but today, you tried to help her snap out of it—and it worked!

You take a mental picture of Jamie's bright face as you step out of the sports center and into the sunlight. You know that the old Jamie is still going to pop up and annoy you now and then. The more you get to know and understand her, though, the more you hope you'll see of *this* Jamie—a fun, talented teammate, and maybe even a friend.

The End

When Amber walks over with Meatloaf, you ask her if she'll take a few pictures of the puppy for you. She's good with dogs, and you hope she can get him to be still and pay attention for a minute.

"Sure!" says Amber, reaching for your camera with her free hand. "Sit, Meatloaf. Sit here and be a good boy."

Unfortunately, before Amber can get Meatloaf to sit, Jamie goes into annoying-Jamie mode—making faces at the puppy and telling him to say "cheese," which gets him all fired up again.

But that changes when you turn your attention toward her. "Hey, Jamie," you say, "I hear you have seven brothers! What's that like?"

Jamie looks surprised by your question—and pleased. It's probably the first one you've ever asked her, and she's more than happy to answer it.

Jamie starts talking about her family, and pretty soon you've learned where she's from (Connecticut), when her birthday is (June 7), what she got for her birthday (roller skates), and what her favorite animal is (butterflies). She actually knows a ton about butterflies. Who knew?

You end up having a pretty decent conversation with Jamie *and* getting some great photos out of the afternoon— thanks to Amber.

 Turn to page 65.

You lift your camera and take a few unposed shots of Meatloaf. When Jamie sees you shooting, she starts goofing around, squatting and making faces behind Meatloaf.

"Jamie, stop—" Amber starts to say.

"It's okay, Amber," you say, "these are great shots! Jamie, can you hold Meatloaf on your lap?"

Jamie seems pleased to be a part of the photo shoot. She scoops Meatloaf onto her lap and rocks him in her arms like a baby.

Click! You catch that shot.

When Meatloaf jumps off Jamie's lap, she reaches for his front paws and starts dancing with him.

Click! Click! You capture that one, too. Too cute!

You also get a shot of Jamie tickling Meatloaf's belly. He wiggles his legs in the air, which inspires Jamie to lie on her back and wiggle her legs in the air, too.

Click! Click! Click! You take more pictures than you thought you would, and each one is cuter than the last. By the end of the hour, you have more than enough photos for your essay, and Jamie and Meatloaf seem to have become fast friends. Your last shot is one of him plastering her chin with kisses.

 Turn to page 68.

You take a deep breath and go on. "Jamie," you say, "why do you think we don't get along better during the school year?"

You steal a glance at Jamie's face, waiting for her response. She looks confused.

"What do you mean?" she asks, stopping in the middle of the path and hugging the volleyball tightly to her chest. "We've always been friends, haven't we?"

You're shocked. *Always been friends?* You have no idea how to respond to that. "Well . . . I mean, we've known each other a long time, but mostly . . . um, we've just fought, haven't we?" you stammer.

Jamie's face falls. She starts to say something, but then she just shrugs and starts walking again. She's totally, painfully silent the rest of the way back to Brightstar House.

 Turn to page 64.

After the water break, Jamie is like a new player on the court. She tries to get to the ball first, and when she does, she always passes it to you for the second hit. Your teacher even compliments her on her passing skills, which Jamie pretends not to hear—but you see the smile spread across her face as she turns back toward the net.

Your teacher compliments you after the game, too. "I don't know what you said to Jamie," she says, "but it worked. You might make a great coach someday."

You feel pretty proud of yourself for figuring out a way to help Jamie shine on the court. You don't know if you and Jamie will ever be great friends, but you *do* make great partners, now that you've gotten to know her better. You're glad you took the time to do that.

The End

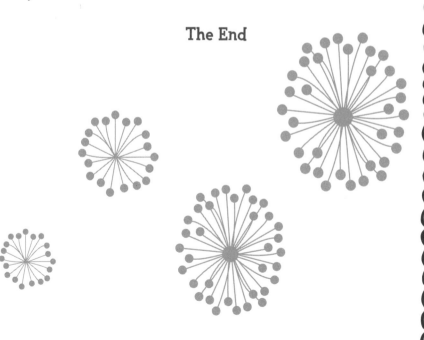

When the two of you get to Jamie's door, you wonder if she'll say something to you or just head inside. You're relieved when she stops walking and turns to you, her cheeks pink.

"I guess I'm just not very good at being friends," she says, her eyes barely meeting yours. "*You* are, though," she adds. "You have a lot of friends."

Jamie's words take you aback, and for some reason, you feel a twinge of guilt. Maybe it's because Jamie's right—you *do* have a lot of friends, but Jamie sure doesn't.

Suddenly, you feel more sorry for her than anything. She looks so sad right now. You wish you could make her feel better, so you do something you never thought you'd do—you reach out and give Jamie a hug.

Turn to page 66.

You're working on your Meatloaf essay later that night when you hear the *ding* of a new e-mail. You're shocked to see that it's from Jamie, who has never e-mailed you before. She must have gotten your address from the campus directory. She writes:

Hey! I had fun with you and Meatloaf today. Maybe we can teach him how to skateboard—I saw a skateboarding bulldog on TV once. Speaking of skating, do you like to roller-skate? Maybe we could go skating around campus sometime.

You stare at Jamie's e-mail for a while, not sure how to respond. A couple of days ago, you would have said no or made up some excuse about being too busy. But today, you had a pretty good time with Jamie. Are you willing to try hanging out with her again?

 If you say yes, turn to page 78.

If you say no, turn to page 67.

When you get back to your own room, you see that you have an e-mail from Megan:

We made it to Florida—finally! And now we're driving down toward the Florida Keys. It's the longest trip ever. My little brother is driving me crazy.

Speaking of crazy, I just heard from Shelby that you and Jamie have been hanging out. Are you like best friends now? I heard she had a caterpillar in her room. I would have expected a PIRANHA. :)

Megan's poking fun at Jamie, and normally, you'd join in with a joke of your own. You can't, though—not after the conversation you just had with Jamie.

You wish you could explain to Megan what Jamie is really like, but you're not sure Megan would understand the way Shelby does. It might be easier to just play along with her. What do you do?

If you respond to Megan with a joke, turn to page 81.

If you defend Jamie, turn to page 69.

Asking Jamie a few questions about herself is a far cry from hanging out with her. You're just not sure that's a good idea. So you e-mail Jamie back and tell her no, that you have to finish your essay, which is due Friday.

You feel good about the way you handled Jamie's invitation, and you think that's the end of that—until Friday arrives, and Jamie sends you another e-mail.

Now that you're done with your essay, how about a little fun? My swimming class is going to a water park off campus tomorrow. Want to come?

You're irritated that Jamie won't let up, and you're tempted to just not respond. But you have to admit, you're kind of interested, too. A trip to a water park sounds like a blast. What do you do?

 If you don't respond to Jamie's e-mail, turn to page 75.

 If you say no to the water park, turn to page 70.

 If you say yes, go online to innerstarU.com/secret and enter this code: BFAIR2OTHERS

You head home that afternoon surprised by how much fun you had and full of excitement about the essay you'll write about Meatloaf—complete with funny photos.

First things first, though. You send some of the photos in an e-mail to Shelby. You want to show her how sweet and silly Meatloaf is. Maybe it'll help change her mind about bulldogs.

As an afterthought, you send the e-mail to Megan and Logan, too, just to show them what you've been up to. Then you get started on your essay.

As you write about Meatloaf, you keep checking the photos for funny details, like Meatloaf's wrinkly brow, or the way his tongue hangs out of his mouth sideways, or how his head seems too big for his body. But you find yourself laughing at Jamie's expressions and poses, too.

Jamie is a pretty funny girl, you realize—at least when she's not using her humor in a mean or annoying way.

 Turn to page 71.

You spend some time thinking about what to say. Then you type this:

Jamie's not that bad, Megan. I've gotten to know her better, and she's actually pretty fun when you spend time with her one-on-one. I hope you'll give her a chance, too.

You're scared to send the e-mail because you don't want things to feel weird between you and Megan. But you remember how sad Jamie looked earlier today, and you decide that you don't want to bad-mouth her anymore.

You quickly click "send." Then you sign out of your e-mail before Megan can respond. You're afraid that she's going to write back something negative, and you're just not ready to deal with that yet.

 Turn to page 72.

You write a short e-mail to Jamie that says:

Thanks for the invite, but I can't do the water park Saturday. Sorry!

Jamie doesn't respond on Friday, but you figure she'll write back with three more invitations over the weekend.

Except she doesn't. As you stare at your empty e-mail in-box on Sunday, are you relieved or disappointed? You can't tell.

One thing's for sure: it's going to be a long summer if you spend your weekends doing nothing but homework. You're going to have to say yes to someone or something, *if* you get another chance.

The End

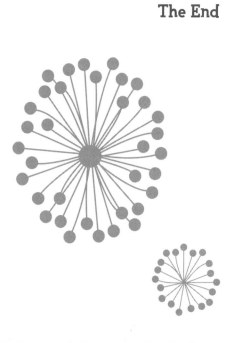

When you hear a *ding,* you check your e-mail, expecting to see something from Shelby. Instead, you see a message from Megan, whom you haven't heard from all week. You're excited to hear about her Florida trip!

When you open the e-mail, though, you see that Megan wrote just one line in response to the pictures you sent her of Meatloaf and Jamie:

Wow . . . a bulldog and a bully! LOL

You think at first that Megan is using the word *bully* the way Amber did—as a nickname for bulldogs. Then you realize she's talking about Jamie.

Is Jamie a bully? you wonder. You used to think so. It's true that she'd do anything for a laugh, and sometimes she takes it too far and can be hurtful.

But talking with Amber—and spending time with Jamie and Meatloaf—has you seeing things in a new light. Maybe, like bulldogs, Jamie is just a little misunderstood.

 Turn to page 74.

Megan never does write back, but things feel a little different between you and Jamie since your e-mail to Megan. For the next couple of weeks, you and Jamie hang out together every day, playing volleyball, doing homework, and swimming at Starfire Lake. Then one morning, Jamie calls you to tell you that Harriet the Caterpillar just made a chrysalis. "You have to see it!" she says.

You rush down the hall to Jamie's room, and sure enough, Harriet's gone. In her place is a greenish-brown sack hanging from a leaf in the aquarium. Jamie has her face pressed to the glass.

"When will she turn into a butterfly?" you ask.

"In a week or two," Jamie whispers, as if she doesn't want to disturb the chrysalis. You can tell that this is a huge deal for her, and you're flattered that she called *you* to share in it.

 Turn to page 80.

You try to get back to writing your essay, but you keep thinking about Megan's e-mail.

You start wondering if maybe your essay can be about *more* than just Meatloaf. You could write about bullies and bulldogs, and how they're both sometimes misunderstood. Or you could write about Meatloaf and Jamie, who both like to clown around and make you laugh.

Either way, it seems as if your essay project just got a lot more interesting.

 If you write about bullies and bulldogs, turn to page 76.

If you write about Meatloaf and Jamie, who both make you laugh, turn to page 77.

You decide not to e-mail Jamie back. Actually, you just put off responding, and all of a sudden it's Saturday, and it's too late to say yes to her invitation. You spend your day doing history homework, but your mind keeps wandering to the water park. Should you have said yes?

By Sunday, boredom is setting in. You wish you had something fun to look forward to. You decide to head over to Pet-Palooza to see if Amber's there, but as you leave your room, you hear Jamie's voice down the hall.

You quickly duck back into your room. You feel bad about not responding to Jamie's invitation. What would you say to her? You should have at least told her no if you weren't going to go.

So you stay in your room and think about your next English assignment: an essay about something that gets your heart pumping. What gets your heart pumping? Guilt, and fear of running into Jamie, obviously.

Oh, well. At least you have good material for your essay. And you might as well get started now.

The End

Your "Bulldogs and Bullies" essay almost writes itself:

I know a bulldog named Meatloaf, and nothing makes me laugh more than Meatloaf's cute, smushy face when he's clowning around. Unfortunately, bulldogs have a bad reputation. Lots of people avoid them because they think they're mean. Bulldogs can be stubborn, but they also can be really sweet and fun to be around, if you just give them a little attention.

I learned that bulldogs are sometimes called "bullies." That's funny, because people who bully are kind of like bulldogs. They like to clown around, too, and can take it too far—and hurt your feelings. But did you know that some people who bully are just trying to tell you they need more attention?

I think that everyone who is afraid of bulldogs should give them a second chance. And if you know someone who takes jokes too far, try to figure out why she does it. Is she just looking for attention—or maybe even a friend? People who bully might need a second chance sometimes, too.

 Turn to page 83.

You decide to call your essay "Clowning Around." You open your essay by saying that you not only laughed a lot during this assignment but that you learned a lot, too. You figure your teacher will like that part, but it's also kind of true.

You go on to say that you learned a lot about bulldogs and your new friend Meatloaf by playing with him. You add that you learned a little bit about a classmate, too—that she was very funny and good with dogs.

You attach a bunch of pictures to the essay so that your teacher can see just how hilarious the photo shoot was. Then you decide to print two more copies of your essay— one for Amber and one for Jamie. They both helped you with this assignment, and you know they'll like seeing the photos.

You don't know what next week will bring. Maybe you'll hang out with Amber and Meatloaf again, or maybe you'll be busy doing other things. But if you see Jamie around campus this summer, you're not going to run in the other direction. You'll actually say hello. You might hang out with her for a while. And you *might* even end up having some fun.

The End

You had a lot of fun with Jamie today, and you do like to roller-skate. In fact, you just got new rainbow-colored wheels that you'd like to try out.

You e-mail Jamie back with a yes, and you meet her the next day out in front of Brightstar House. When Jamie sees your new wheels, she does a double-take. "Cool," she says.

You're about to thank her for the compliment when she says, "I mean, they're not as cool as mine, but . . . they're not bad." She gives you a sideways grin and then starts skating down the path.

You follow Jamie, winding around the bumpy stone path that runs up to the student center, through the patio of the art studios, around the star garden in front of the nature center, and down through Five-Points Plaza.

Jamie cracks you up all the way. Sometimes she's trying to be funny, like when she pretends to have wobbly legs while she skates. Sometimes she's just *naturally* funny, like when she widens her legs to clear a stick in the path and ends up doing the splits in the grass. By the time you get back to Brightstar House, you're both breathing hard and giggling. What a blast!

 Turn to page 82.

A week and a half later, there's still no sign of Harriet the Butterfly, but the chrysalis is different—it's darker now, as if the wings of the butterfly are showing through.

When Jamie invites you to stay over that night "to watch and wait for Harriet," you agree. You pack your camera in your duffel, just in case.

You and Jamie stay up late, watching a movie and trying to keep tabs on the chrysalis at the same time. When your eyelids grow heavy, you both reluctantly go to sleep. Jamie clutches Cuddles and a flashlight so that she can check on Harriet every now and then.

You wake up in the morning to Jamie shaking your shoulder. "Look!" she says, pointing toward the aquarium. And there she is! Harriet doesn't look like Harriet anymore. She has black and white wings with brilliant reddish-orange spots on the tips. She's slowly opening and closing her wet wings.

 Turn to page 86.

You type the first thing that comes into your mind:

Jamie doesn't have a piranha, but she DOES sleep with a crocodile named Cuddles.

As soon as you click "send," you regret what you wrote. Cuddles might be something Jamie doesn't want other people to know about. You wish you could take back your words, but you've already sent them out into cyberspace. It's on days like this that you think you should just avoid e-mail altogether.

You hope Megan will just laugh at the joke and then let it go, but she doesn't. She writes back the next day and sends an attachment: a photo of a crocodile she saw in Everglades National Park. She adds a caption: "Cuddles the Crocodile, Jamie's BFF."

The photo would be funny if joking around about Jamie and her stuffed animal didn't make you feel so guilty. You delete Megan's e-mail without responding.

 Turn to page 85.

A few days later, you get a new English assignment to write an essay about something that gets your heart pumping. You figure that skating fits that bill, so you call Jamie and invite her to join you on the roller-skating paths again.

Jamie beats you downstairs to the lobby of Brightstar House. When you get there, you're surprised to see that she's carrying a new pair of skates. Actually, they aren't new skates. They just have new wheels—rainbow-colored wheels.

"Nice wheels," you point out.

"Thanks," Jamie says. "I'd actually been thinking about buying those for ages. You just beat me to the punch."

For ages? you think. You know that Girl Gear, the sports shop on campus, just got the wheels in last week—the clerk told you so. You don't really mind that Jamie's wheels are just like yours. But does she have to make up stories about them?

 Turn to page 84.

After you reread your essay, you decide *not* to attach a picture of Meatloaf and Jamie. You don't want your teacher or anyone else to see Jamie's photo and know your essay is partly about her.

You do e-mail a few of the pictures to Jamie, though. She helped you with your homework assignment, after all—and showed you a different way of looking at things. Maybe, by keeping an open mind and giving her a chance, you can help her in some ways, too.

The End

You try to shake off your irritation with Jamie and focus on having a good time with her. It's not hard—the sun is shining, there's a cool breeze blowing, and skating paths stretch out far in front of you.

This time you and Jamie skate toward the Market, which is a maze of colorful tents and tables displaying things to buy. You skate slowly through the clusters of shoppers. Jamie does, too, but she hams it up for you, pretending to nearly wipe out over and over again—and occasionally succeeding!

You stop at a jewelry table to catch your breath and maybe to do a little shopping.

"Ooh, look at this!" you say to Jamie. You pick up a funky silver ring with a blue marble on top. When you slide it on your finger, you're shocked to see that it fits perfectly.

"You should get it," Jamie urges.

You agree. But while you're fishing in your pocket to find money, you see Jamie reach for a ring, too—one that looks *just* like yours. *Really?* you think. *What a copycat!*

You pay for your ring and then skate to a nearby bench. You're not surprised to see Jamie pay for her ring, too, just a moment later.

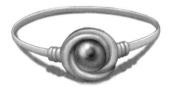 Turn to page 88.

Unfortunately, Megan *doesn't* delete the photo. She sends it to Shelby, Logan, and lots of other Innerstar U students.

Logan e-mails the whole group to point out that the crocodile in the photo is actually an alligator. (Leave it to super-smart Logan to know the difference.) But Shelby e-mails a note directly to you:

Does Jamie know about this photo? If not, you should tell her. If it gets forwarded to her, it'll hurt her feelings.

You stare at Shelby's words, trying to figure out what to do. Shelby's probably right—you should tell Jamie. But what if she gets mad at you for telling Megan about Cuddles the Crocodile? You doubt that Jamie has seen the e-mail yet—and hope that she never will.

 If you tell Jamie about the e-mail, turn to page 90.

If you don't, turn to page 92.

For a while, you and Jamie watch Harriet in wonder.
Then it dawns on you that Jamie is going to have to let
Harriet go soon. You offer to go with her—and Jamie
gratefully agrees.

Late that afternoon, you help Jamie carry the aquarium
to sunny Morningstar Meadow. When Jamie takes the lid
off Harriet's aquarium, the butterfly crawls toward the open
air. She hesitates on the edge of the aquarium, flapping her
wings slowly, and then she takes flight.

Harriet lands first on Jamie's hand. You snap a picture
with your camera before the butterfly flaps her wings again
and darts off into the sunlight.

Jamie glances skyward for a while, until she seems sure that Harriet is gone. Then the two of you walk back toward your rooms slowly—without talking.

Jamie is probably thinking about Harriet. But you? You're thinking that it's almost August. There are only two weeks left before the rest of your friends come back. And where will that leave Jamie? You wish you could do something for her.

 If you frame a photo of Harriet for Jamie, turn to page 93.

 If you e-mail your friends to ask them to give Jamie a chance, turn to page 89.

When Jamie skates over and sits down beside you, she's smiling and already wearing her ring. She holds it up to show you.

"Look," she says. "It matches the new pin I just bought." Jamie holds her ring finger near a silver pin on her shirt, which is shaped like a small roller skate. It's actually pretty cute.

You're still annoyed about the ring, though. You sit together silently for a moment, and Jamie finally asks, "What's wrong?"

If you tell Jamie what's wrong, turn to page 91.

If you keep it to yourself, turn to page 94.

You decide to e-mail the photo of Harriet to Shelby, Megan, Logan, and some of your other friends. You want to share that magical moment with them, but there's something else you want more—you want them to realize that just like Harriet, Jamie has changed, too.

Along with the photo, you send a short e-mail:

Jamie and I released her butterfly today. I've had a lot of fun with Jamie this summer. She seems different somehow, and we've become friends. Anyway, can't wait to see you all soon!

It's not much, but maybe it's a start at paving the way for some new friendships for Jamie. You click "send" and watch the e-mail icon on your computer screen flap its wings and take flight.

The End

You wait until after volleyball practice to tell Jamie about the e-mail. As you walk toward the student center to get smoothies, you open your mouth and start talking, crossing your fingers behind your back in the hopes that Jamie won't be *too* mad. You tell her how you sort of mentioned Cuddles the Crocodile to Megan, and how she sort of got carried away with it in her e-mails to other friends.

Jamie stops walking. She suddenly looks like the old Jamie—her face screwed up, searching for something hurtful to say. But instead of flinging an insult at you, she tosses you the volleyball—hard—and walks away. Halfway down the path toward Brightstar House, Jamie breaks into a jog.

You feel sick to your stomach, but you're also glad the conversation is over. Will Jamie forgive you? You're not sure. The ball's in her court now.

Actually, you think as you glance down at the volleyball in your hands, *it's in mine.* You may have to work a little harder for Jamie's forgiveness. Are you willing to do that?

 If you try to make amends with Jamie, turn to page 95.

 If you wait for her to come to you, turn to page 99.

You blurt out the truth before you can change your mind. "I just don't know why you keep *copying* me, Jamie," you say. "First with the rainbow-colored skate wheels and now with the ring. It's really annoying."

Jamie looks as if you just slapped her across the face. You probably could have been a little less harsh, you realize, now that the words are out.

Jamie's face is beet red. When she finds her own words, she spews them at you. "First of all," she says, "I can buy whatever I want. I don't need permission from you. And second, who would want to copy *you*, anyway? You're so full of yourself!"

Jamie pushes off from the bench and starts skating away from you—too fast, you can already tell. You're not surprised when she takes a corner too sharply and ends up flat on her face on the cobblestone. You *are* surprised when she lies there and doesn't get up.

 Turn to page 108.

You can't bring yourself to tell Jamie about Megan's e-mail. Things are going well between you and Jamie this summer. If she finds out that you shared a secret of hers, she may not want to hang out with you anymore.

You focus instead on getting to know Jamie better—and making the most of the weeks you have left. You swim together at the lake and play beach volleyball. You discover that you both love roller-skating, so you explore campus on wheels. And when Harriet the Caterpillar hatches into Harriet the Butterfly, you head to the meadow together to set her free.

By the end of the summer, Jamie has become a true friend. But when you turn the calendar page and see that your other friends are coming back to Innerstar U soon, you worry about what they'll think about your new friendship with Jamie. Will they understand? Will they try to accept Jamie as a friend, too?

 Turn to page 96.

Your photo of Harriet turns out pretty well. You print, frame, and wrap it, and then give it to Jamie on the last day of volleyball class. When she unwraps the photo, she smiles and sighs.

"Oh, Harriet," she says. "I miss her already, don't you?"

You nod and put your arm around Jamie's shoulder, which feels much more natural now.

Jamie traces the frame with her fingertip, as if trying to find the right words to say. Then she looks up at you and says simply, "Thank you. This has been my best summer at Innerstar U."

You smile and give Jamie a hug. But then you realize what her words mean. "Wait," you say. "You've spent other summers here, too?"

Jamie nods. "I spend every summer here," she says, staring at the picture frame. "My mom travels for work during the summer, so it's easier if my brothers and I just stay at school."

 Turn to page 98.

You bite your tongue. You don't want to get into it with Jamie. "Nothing's wrong," you say, trying to keep your voice light. "I'm just worried about my history homework. Maybe we should head back to Brightstar House."

Jamie shrugs. "Okay," she says, standing up from the bench.

You and Jamie skate back across campus in silence. When you get to your room, you immediately sit down at your desk and e-mail Shelby. Writing about what's going on with Jamie helps you sort it all out somehow. You type this:

I got new wheels for my roller skates, and Jamie bought the same wheels. I bought a new ring, and Jamie bought the SAME ring. She's copying everything I do. What's up with that???

 Turn to page 119.

You want things to be okay between you and Jamie, so you go back to your room and dig through your bedcovers to find your own version of Cuddles—an old rabbit named Joe. He's been yours since you were two, and you sleep with him every night. You never bring him to sleepovers, but you think it's time for Joe to take a trip out into the light.

You knock on Jamie's door, and you're relieved when she answers it.

"Jamie, I was wrong," you say quickly, before she can shut the door in your face. "I never should have told anyone about Cuddles. If it makes you feel better, I have a secret friend, too. Jamie, meet Joe."

Jamie hesitates for a moment, and then she smiles and reaches out to shake Joe's foot. At that moment, you know you did the right thing by coming here to apologize. You're sure of something else, too—that you and Jamie have formed a true friendship, a friendship worth protecting.

The End

A few days before your friends are due to return to Innerstar U, you get an e-mail from Shelby that reads:

I can't believe summer's over already! Mom is dropping me off at Brightstar House around 3:00 on Friday. Meet me there? Can't wait to see you!

Hearing from Shelby makes you excited about seeing her again.

As for Megan? You haven't heard from her since she e-mailed you the crocodile photo. That was more than a month ago. You're hoping she'll have forgotten all about Cuddles the Crocodile by now.

On Friday, just before Shelby is due to arrive, you invite Jamie to wait with you in the lobby of Brightstar House. The two of you find seats by the front door, and when you see a girl walk through that door wearing a green beret over her dark curls, you jump up to give your friend a hug. It feels so good to see Shelby again!

She seems just as happy to see you, but when she notices Jamie by your side, you catch the flash of surprise in her eyes. She quickly covers it up, though, and says hi to Jamie. That's Shelby—the queen of second chances.

 Turn to page 104.

You're shocked. You felt so sorry for yourself when you realized you'd have to stay behind at Innerstar U for a whole summer. You can't even imagine what it would feel like if you had to stay here *every* summer, as Jamie does.

"I'm sorry," you say.

Jamie shrugs and smiles. "It's no big deal," she says. "I'm used to it. Besides, this summer wasn't too bad. I hatched a California Sister butterfly, and I sort of made a friend."

Jamie grins at you, and you smile back. You really *have* become friends. Summer may be ending soon, but your friendship with Jamie doesn't have to—not if you take care of it.

🌟 Turn to page 101.

Jamie's mad, but you figure she just needs time to stew. You don't reach out to her over the weekend.

When Monday comes, though, you're looking forward to volleyball, and you hope that everything will be okay between the two of you. You're shocked to walk into the gym and see that Jamie has already partnered up with someone else.

Suddenly, you're the odd girl out. You do a couple of partner drills with the teacher, which is embarrassing. All the while, you keep glancing Jamie's way, hoping she'll give you a smile. She doesn't.

Can I blame her, though? you wonder as you walk back to your room after class. At the start of the summer, you were so worried about whether Jamie was someone who could be trusted. Turns out *you* were the one who couldn't be.

It may take a while to earn back Jamie's trust, but you're surprised by how willing you are now to try. Good thing you have a few more weeks of summer ahead.

The End

You don't have to wait long. The next afternoon, you meet Jamie for a smoothie at the student center. You order a strawberry-mango smoothie, and Jamie—in line behind you—orders exactly the same thing.

You fight the urge to call her on it. *It's a compliment,* you remind yourself. To fight your irritation with Jamie, you decide to pay her a compliment back.

 If you compliment Jamie on her skating ability,
turn to page 107.

 If you compliment her on her sense of humor,
turn to page 112.

 If you compliment her on her silver skate pin,
turn to page 102.

You wish you could plan something special with Jamie—a sort of mini vacation for the girl who never gets to go away for the summer. You talk with the staff at the nature center about renting a tent that you can pitch by Starfire Lake. You talk with your volleyball teacher about setting up a net on the beach, or even in shallow water. Then you talk with Jamie about the idea. She loves it—she can hardly wait!

You decide to hold this campout at the end of summer break and to invite all your friends, who should be back from vacation by then. Maybe if they spend a night camping and playing volleyball with the "new Jamie," she'll make a few friends before school starts.

You e-mail out invitations listing Jamie and you as hosts. And then you watch and wait as the RSVP e-mails start coming in.

Shelby responds with a "yes" right away—no surprise there. So does Logan. A few more "yes's" trickle in over the week. But by Friday, you still haven't heard from Megan.

 Turn to page 103.

You point toward Jamie's skate pin. "Nice pin," you say. "I didn't get the chance to tell you that the other day."

Jamie looks down at her pin. "Do you really like it?" she asks, studying your face. She seems satisfied that you're telling the truth, because she goes on to say, "That's good, because I got one for you, too!"

She pulls a wrapped box out of her pocket and sets it on the table in front of you. There's a tag on top that reads "To remind you of our summer on wheels."

"Wow, Jamie, that's so nice," you say, feeling guilty that just moments ago, you were annoyed with her.

"Well, open it and put it on," Jamie urges. "With our matching wheels, rings, and pins, we'll be like the Skating Sisters. Of course, I'll still be faster."

When you look up, there's a twinkle in Jamie's eye, but something else, too—an invitation for friendship, maybe?

You carefully pin the silver skate to the front of your T-shirt. You figure that it's your way of saying, "I'm having fun, too, and I'm willing to try."

The End

And then, finally, it comes. When you open up Megan's e-mail, you see three short words:

I'll be there.

Megan doesn't write anything else, but you don't care. If you can just get Megan to give Jamie a chance at the campout, maybe it'll get the ball rolling. Maybe you can *all* be friends.

And if not? you ask yourself. *What if it doesn't work?*

You're tempted to e-mail Shelby for reassurance, but you don't. Instead, you sit back for a moment and try to imagine what Shelby would say. She would say something wise, such as, "You can't make people be friends with each other. You can only choose friends for yourself."

Yup, that's what she'd say, you think with a giggle. *And she'd be right.*

Shelby's a great friend, and so is Jamie. You've chosen well.

The End

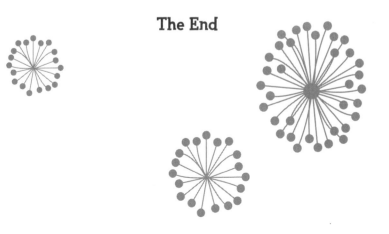

The three of you are sitting at dinner that night when Megan finally gets back from vacation. She waves to you from the cafeteria line, but when she sees Jamie sitting beside you, her jaw drops.

Megan is quiet throughout dinner. When Jamie gets up to go check out dessert, Megan nudges you. "What gives?" she asks. "Why are you hanging out with her?"

You glance toward Shelby for support, and she jumps right in to save you.

"They're *friends*," Shelby says to Megan—as if it's the most obvious thing in the world. Then she tries to change the subject.

But Megan won't let it go. "Friends with Jamie?" she says sharply. "More like frenemies."

"I heard that," says Jamie from behind her. There's an edge in her voice that you haven't heard in a long time.

Megan's cheeks flush, but she doesn't back down. "That's okay," she says loudly. "It's the truth."

You want to crawl under the table, but both Megan and Jamie are staring at you, waiting for you to do something. To do what: choose sides?

If you speak up, turn to page 110.

If you stay out of it, turn to page 106.

You don't want to get involved, so you say nothing. But your silence seems to fuel the fire between Jamie and Megan.

Jamie takes a step toward Megan. "The truth is," she says pointedly, "things were a lot more fun around here this summer without *you*."

Megan snaps right back at her. "Don't be such a *baby*, Jamie," she says. "Why don't you go suck your thumb and cuddle with your stuffed crocodile?"

You drop your fork. You can't believe Megan went there!

Jamie's dark eyes flash toward you, and now you see hurt in those eyes mingled with anger. Before you can say anything, she whirls around and storms out of the cafeteria.

Turn to page 111.

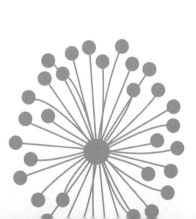

"Did you skate here?" you ask Jamie. It's a silly question—you see her skates peeking out of her duffel bag.

When she nods, you say, "You're really good. You're a great athlete."

Jamie coughs on a mouthful of smoothie. "Well, thanks," she says, reaching for a napkin. Then she cracks a joke, as usual. "I'll bet you wish you were as good as me. I could teach you a few tricks."

There's an awkward silence after that, and finally Jamie adds, "You know, my skating has actually gotten better this summer because of you."

You glance up. *Wow.* You don't recognize this Jamie. She's being so serious—and nice. Did you bring that on by paying her a compliment?

You're learning a lot about Jamie, thanks to Shelby and Amber, who taught you to ask the right questions and give things a chance. So as you finish your smoothie, you ask Jamie one more question: "Do you want to go skating this afternoon? Maybe you *can* teach me a few tricks."

Jamie grins. She doesn't hesitate for a second before giving you a hearty "yes!"

The End

"Jamie!" you call as you skate toward her as fast as you can. You make a not-very-elegant stop and kneel beside her, touching her arm. "Jamie? Are you hurt?"

To your relief, Jamie shakes her head no. But as she quickly turns her face away from yours, you can see that she's crying.

You help Jamie sit up and scooch to the edge of the courtyard, away from shoppers. Her elbow is skinned, but she's okay otherwise—except that the marble on her new ring is chipped.

As Jamie stares at the ring, she makes a confession, which is kind of hard to understand through her tears and sniffles. "Maybe I w-was copying you," she says. "But isn't that what friends do? You and Shelby are always wearing matching friendship bracelets or s-something."

🌟 Turn to page 116.

"Jamie's my friend," you say firmly to Megan. Her face darkens, so you add quickly, "But you're my friend, too. And I'd really like to keep it that way."

Megan stares at you for a long, hard moment, and then she looks down and starts fiddling with her napkin.

When Jamie returns with a chocolate brownie, Megan pretty much ignores her. Eventually, though, Megan starts talking with Shelby again and acting halfway normal.

You breathe a sigh of relief. *Crisis averted*, you think to yourself. *At least for now.*

 Turn to page 114.

Megan seems pretty satisfied with herself, until she sees the look on your face. "What?" she asks, raising her hands in the air. "Jamie had that coming."

You shake your head but say nothing. You're mad at Megan, but you're even angrier at yourself—for breaking Jamie's trust and telling Megan about Cuddles.

You don't finish your dinner—you couldn't eat right now if you tried. You just hurt a friend, and the only thing that you can do is apologize and try to make it right.

As you leave the student center and hurry toward Jamie's room, you think about how differently you feel about Jamie *now* than you did at the start of the summer. You decided way back then to gave Jamie a second chance, and you're really glad you did. You only hope that she'll do the same for you.

The End

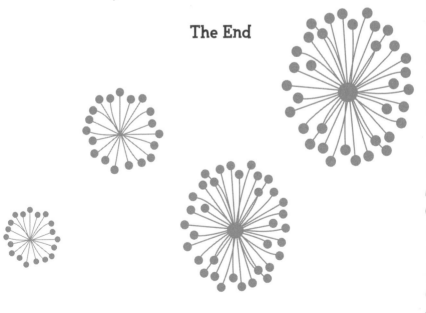

When Jamie takes a big drink of smoothie and shows off her red strawberry-mango mustache, you giggle—and take the opportunity to compliment her on her sense of humor.

"You're hilarious, Jamie," you say. "You're really funny. You know that?"

Jamie's cheeks turn pink, and she takes a small bow. "Thanks," she says. "It's about all I have going for me, so I have to really work it."

You can't tell if she's being serious about that or joking again. "What do you mean?" you ask. "You have plenty going for you."

Jamie shakes her head. "You know what I mean," she says. "I'm not super smart, like Logan. And I'm not super popular, like Shelby—and you."

Popular? You never thought of yourself that way, but you don't argue the point right now. You're more concerned about hearing Jamie kind of put herself down.

 Turn to page 115.

After dinner, as you walk back toward Brightstar House, Shelby praises you for the way you handled the situation between Megan and Jamie. "You didn't choose sides," she says. "You were fair, and you were a good friend."

Shelby's words make you feel a little more hopeful. You don't know if Megan and Jamie will ever get along, but you're proud that you stood up for your friends—your new friend *and* your old friend. And you're grateful to Shelby for being the best friend of all, the one who always gives great advice—and second chances.

The End

A fair friend doesn't choose sides.

"You're plenty smart," you tell Jamie. "You couldn't come up with such funny jokes if you weren't."

Jamie cocks her head and thinks about that. "Okay, maybe I'm *sort* of smart," she says with a smirk. "But I'm definitely not popular." She shrugs and takes another sip of smoothie.

You feel as if you should say something to make Jamie feel better, but what?

 If you give Jamie a tip about popularity, turn to page 117.

 If you try to crack a joke, turn to page 118.

Suddenly, you get it. Jamie was copying you because she wanted to be *friends* with you. What she did was annoying, but her reasons for it were actually pretty sweet.

You think about that for a moment while Jamie wipes her nose on her sleeve and struggles to stand up.

"Jamie, wait," you say, reaching for her hand. When she sits back down, you say, "Friends do try to match each other sometimes. And sometimes they give each other gifts." You slide the new, unchipped ring off your finger and offer it to Jamie. "I want you to have this—a gift from me to you."

Jamie smiles and reaches for the ring. The gift seems to mean a lot to her, or maybe it's the promise of friendship that makes her smile. Whatever the reason, she looks happier now. She slides the ring onto her finger, stands up, and offers you a hand.

As you skate back across campus behind Jamie, you realize that she's not so different from anybody else. She just wants to have a friend and be a friend. She may not always go about it in the best of ways, but at least she's trying. And she's teaching you something about friendship, too—how to slow down and not judge someone's actions too quickly.

When Jamie starts skating with her "wobbly legs" again, you laugh loudly and wiggle your legs, too. This is turning out to be a pretty fun summer. Who knew?

The End

You decide to be honest with Jamie and give her some straight-up advice. "Sometimes," you say, "the best way to make friends isn't through jokes. It's through kindness."

Jamie winces, as if your comment kind of stung. So you quickly add, "You *do* know how to be kind and be a friend, Jamie. You're doing it right now."

Jamie looks as if she's not quite sure you're telling the truth. So you try again, this time speaking Jamie's language. You take a big gulp of smoothie and flash her your own strawberry-mango mustache. "Seriously," you say to Jamie. "I mean it."

Jamie cracks up. But you think she heard your words and that she feels a little bit better about herself. As her new friend, that makes *you* feel pretty good, too.

The End

"So what if you're not the most popular girl on the planet?" you say to Jamie. "I'm not very funny. You want to hear my best joke?"

Jamie smiles. "Bring it on," she says.

"Okay, here goes," you say, rubbing your palms together. "Why were the two little strawberries crying?"

Jamie rolls her eyes. "Because their parents were in a jam," she says. "Oldest joke in the book."

You raise your hands in the air. "Well?" you say. "It's the best I've got." Then you say to Jamie, "I'll make you a deal. I'll teach you what I know about making friends if you teach me what you know about telling jokes."

Jamie makes a funny face, as if she's pondering the question, and then she reaches out her hand. "Deal," she says with a grin.

It's going to be an interesting summer, you think as you squeeze Jamie's hand. English. History. Volleyball. Roller-skating. Joke telling. And friendship—with Jamie. Bring it on.

The End

Shelby e-mails back immediately. Hurrah! She writes:

Think of it this way—when Jamie copies you, it's kind of a compliment to you. It means that she likes your style! I'll bet she wishes she were a little more like you.

Leave it to Shelby to put a positive spin on such an annoying situation. But her words make you think. You decide that from now on, if Jamie copies you, you're going to *try* to take it as a compliment.

 Turn to page 100.